MAPWOR

Activities to Develop Map Skills and Geographical Awareness

GRADES 4-8

WRITTEN BY
PAMELA AMICK KLAWITTER, ED.D.

ILLUSTRATED BY CAROL KRIEGER

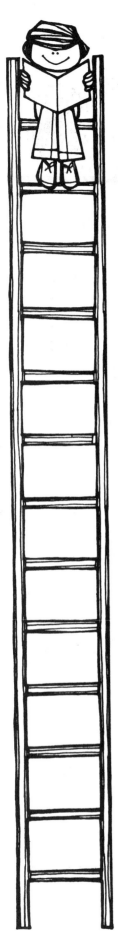

The Learning Works

Edited by Phyllis Amerikaner

Copyright © 1992 by The Learning Works, Inc.

The Learning Works, Inc.
P.O. Box 6187
Santa Barbara, California   93160

pages 44-45 used with permission
The Teacher's Pet
The Learning Works, Inc. — ©1983

Library of Congress Catalog Card Number: 92-81914
ISBN 0-88160-206-X
LW 254

Printed in the United States of America.

Current Printing (last digit): 10 9 8 7 6 5 4 3 2 1

Contents

Introduction

Mapworks is designed to help students develop map skills and geographical awareness. The activities in this book encourage students to use a variety of reference materials, such as almanacs, atlases, encyclopedias, globes, maps, and world record books.

The **Mapworks** activities are divided into four sections. The first section focuses on **United States geography**, the second on **Canadian geography**, and the final two sections on **world geography**. At the end of the book is a convenient, reproducible chart to keep track of the **Mapworks** pages each student completes. The outline map of the world which follows the chart may be used to have students identify continents and oceans. The final pages of the book contain a comprehensive answer key.

In completing the **Mapworks** activities, students will locate over five hundred bodies of water, cities, continents, countries, deserts, islands, mountains, and states. Students will learn to use compass directions, latitude and longitude coordinates, map indexes, and map scales.

Mapworks can do more than help students develop skills in reading maps and in utilizing resource materials. **Mapworks** can also make children aware of the places they learn about in current events, history, literature, and social studies. Having fun with **Mapworks** can make studying geography an exciting challenge, turning *map work* into *map play!*

Given the rapid changes taking place in the world as **Mapworks** went to press, every effort was made to reflect the most up-to-date information possible, including the breakup of the former Soviet Union and of Yugoslavia. Also, since many foreign place names have more than one acceptable spelling, only the most common and easily recognized spelling has been provided.

Which State Am I?

Each statement below describes a U.S. state. Use a map of the United States or an encyclopedia to help you identify the state. Write the name of the state on the line next to its description.

1. I am home to the Black Hills and Sioux Falls. _____

2. Puget Sound is in my northwestern corner. _____

3. Most of Yellowstone National Park lies within my borders. _____

4. My capital city is Dover. _____

5. Lake Okeechobee is my largest lake. _____

6. I touch Lake Michigan and Lake Superior but none of the other Great Lakes. _____

7. I border only one other state. _____

8. Kodiak Island lies off my southern coast. _____

9. I am the only state to touch both the Atlantic Ocean and two of the Great Lakes. _____

10. I separate New Hampshire from Connecticut. _____

11. I am home to Death Valley, the lowest point in the United States. _____

12. I border the Canadian provinces of British Columbia and Saskatchewan. _____

13. Eight states touch my borders. _____

14. I am home to the Grand Canyon. _____

15. I touch the Gulf of Mexico and the Mississippi River but not Texas. _____

Neighborly Trios

Each trio of states listed below shares a border with a fourth state. Use a map of the United States to help you identify the missing state.

1. Idaho, Nevada, Washington _____

2. Illinois, Indiana, Missouri _____

3. Kansas, Nebraska, Wyoming _____

4. Arizona, Idaho, Nevada _____

5. Colorado, South Dakota, Wyoming _____

6. Iowa, North Dakota, Wisconsin _____

7. Kentucky, Maryland, Ohio _____

8. Louisiana, Mississippi, Oklahoma _____

9. Iowa, Montana, Nebraska _____

10. Maine, Massachusetts, Vermont _____

11. Indiana, Iowa, Wisconsin _____

12. Montana, Nevada, Wyoming _____

13. Alabama, South Carolina, Tennessee _____

14. Indiana, Kentucky, Pennsylvania _____

15. Florida, Georgia, Mississippi _____

Name _____

On Opposite Sides

Use a map of the United States to identify the river that forms the border between the states listed below. Write the name of the river on the line beside each pair of states.

1. Arkansas and Tennessee   _____

2. Arizona and California   _____

3. Illinois and Missouri   _____

4. Louisiana and Texas   _____

5. Indiana and Kentucky   _____

6. Minnesota and North Dakota   _____

7. Maryland and Virginia   _____

8. New Jersey and Pennsylvania   _____

9. New Hampshire and Vermont   _____

10. Georgia and South Carolina   _____

11. Oregon and Washington   _____

12. Illinois and Indiana   _____

13. Idaho and Oregon   _____

14. Oklahoma and Texas   _____

15. Iowa and Nebraska   _____

Name _____

Count Me Out

Only two of the three locations in each list below are in the state that is named. Use a detailed map of each state to find the locations in the list. Cross out the one that does *not* belong.

1. **Alaska**   Bristol Bay/Brooks Range/Devils Tower

2. **Connecticut**   Chesapeake Bay/Housatonic River/Thames River

3. **Georgia**   Chattahoochee River/Mobile Bay/Okefenokee Swamp

4. **Hawaii**   Lake Winnebago/Haleakala Crater/Mauna Kea

5. **Louisiana**   Lake Pontchartrain/Red River/White Sands National Monument

6. **Maine**   Cape Cod/Kennebec River/Moosehead Lake

7. **Michigan**   Mackinac Island/Mesabi Range/Muskegon River

8. **New Hampshire**   Green Mountains/Mount Washington/White Mountains

9. **New Mexico**   Carlsbad Caverns/Rio Grande/Zion National Park

10. **New York**   Acadia National Park/Catskill Mountains/Finger Lakes

11. **North Carolina** Badlands/Blue Ridge Mountains/Cape Hatteras

12. **Pennsylvania**   Grand Coulee Dam/Pocono Mountains/Susquehanna River

13. **Texas**   Galveston Bay/Ouachita Mountains/Pecos River

14. **Virginia**   James River/Pamlico Sound/Shenandoah National Park

15. **Washington**   Flathead Lake/Klickitat River/Mount Rainier

Name _____

Capital Anagrams

> An **anagram** is a word or phrase that is created by rearranging all of the letters of another word or phrase. For example, one anagram of the word *Salem* is *males*. Another is *meals*.

The words and phrases below are anagrams for the names of U.S. state capitals. Unscramble the anagrams. Write the name of the capital city in the first column and the name of the state in the second column. Use the city names listed in the box below as clues, but be careful. You will not need *all* of them.

	Capital City	**State**
1. brim sack	_____	_____
2. shrug briar	_____	_____
3. vain shell	_____	_____
4. trickle lot	_____	_____
5. age run boot	_____	_____
6. covered pin	_____	_____
7. a plain son	_____	_____
8. at a sea shell	_____	_____
9. to scare man	_____	_____
10. lion said pain	_____	_____
11. net pro lime	_____	_____
12. Kathy I am cool	_____	_____

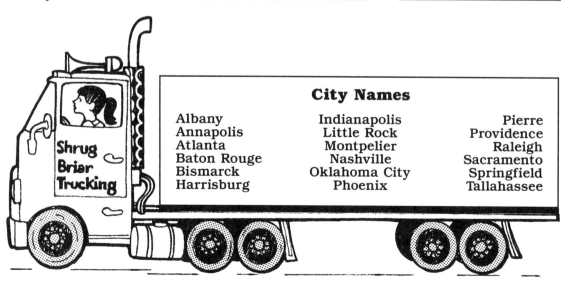

City Names

Albany	Indianapolis	Pierre
Annapolis	Little Rock	Providence
Atlanta	Montpelier	Raleigh
Baton Rouge	Nashville	Sacramento
Bismarck	Oklahoma City	Springfield
Harrisburg	Phoenix	Tallahassee

Name _____

Which Way?

Use a map of the United States to find each of the pairs of locations listed below. Determine which way you would have to travel to get from the first place in the pair to the other. Use the abbreviations in the box when you write your answers.

Directions			
N North	**S** South	**E** East	**W** West
NE Northeast	**NW** Northwest	**SE** Southeast	**SW** Southwest

Which way would I travel to get from

1. Louisiana to Colorado? _____

2. Alabama to Virginia? _____

3. Florida to Nebraska? _____

4. Arizona to Utah? _____

5. Oregon to New Mexico? _____

6. Kentucky to Texas? _____

7. New York to Arkansas? _____

8. Wisconsin to Lake Michigan? _____

9. Hawaii to California? _____

10. Colorado to Utah? _____

11. Chicago to Atlanta? _____

12. New Orleans to Nashville? _____

13. Milwaukee to Minneapolis? _____

14. Seattle to Denver? _____

15. Pikes Peak to Mount Whitney? _____

Name _____

Where Am I?

To help us find where places are on the earth, mapmakers have created a system of lines. Map lines that run east and west are called **lines of latitude**. Lines of latitude measure the distance north or south of the **equator**, which is 0 ° latitude. Map lines that run north and south are called **lines of longitude**. Lines of longitude measure the distance east or west of the **prime meridian**, which is 0 ° longitude.

Use a map of the United States or a globe to locate the state in which each latitude-longitude combination intersects.

	Name of State	**Latitude**	**Longitude**
1.	_____	30 ° N	85 ° W
2.	_____	45 ° N	100 ° W
3.	_____	60 ° N	160 ° W
4.	_____	35 ° N	95 ° W
5.	_____	45 ° N	120 ° W
6.	_____	35 ° N	105 ° W
7.	_____	40 ° N	95 ° W
8.	_____	40 ° N	115 ° W
9.	_____	35 ° N	80 ° W
10.	_____	45 ° N	95 ° W
11.	_____	45 ° N	70 ° W
12.	_____	40 ° N	80 ° W
13.	_____	45 ° N	115 ° W
14.	_____	40 ° N	85 ° W
15.	_____	45 ° N	90 ° W

Name _____

Miles to Go

Using a **map scale** is a way of estimating distances between points on a map. Most maps are small in comparison to the area they represent. Maps are drawn "to scale," so that the distance on the map corresponds to a specific distance on the earth. For example, one inch on a map might represent one hundred miles on the earth.

Use a ruler to measure the distance on a map between each of the pairs of cities below. Use the map scale to convert this distance to miles. Circle the number of miles which is closest to the actual distance between the cities.

Approximately how many miles is it from

1. Denver, Colorado, to Omaha, Nebraska?	100	300	500
2. Chattanooga, Tennessee, to Little Rock, Arkansas?	400	600	800
3. St. Paul, Minnesota, to Salt Lake City, Utah?	600	800	1,000
4. Carson City, Nevada, to Santa Fe, New Mexico?	600	800	1,000
5. Augusta, Maine, to Columbus, Ohio?	550	750	950
6. Lansing, Michigan, to Pierre, South Dakota?	400	600	800
7. Boise, Idaho, to Cheyenne, Wyoming?	400	600	800
8. Harrisburg, Pennsylvania, to Indianapolis, Indiana?	500	700	900
9. Austin, Texas, to Montgomery, Alabama?	300	500	700
10. Atlanta, Georgia, to Santa Fe, New Mexico?	1,050	1,250	1,450
11. Olympia, Washington, to Sacramento, California?	600	800	1,000
12. Albany, New York, to Madison, Wisconsin?	400	600	800

Name _____

Ten are True

Only ten of the fifteen statements below are true. Use a map of Canada to determine whether each statement is correct. If the statement is **true**, circle the letter **T**. If the statement is **false**, circle the letter **F**.

T   F   1. Great Bear Lake lies northwest of Great Slave Lake.

T   F   2. James Bay is located between the provinces of Quebec and Ontario.

T   F   3. Vancouver is the capital of British Columbia.

T   F   4. The cities of Montreal and Quebec are on the St. Lawrence River.

T   F   5. Ontario extends farther south than any other province.

T   F   6. The capital of Prince Edward Island is Charlottetown.

T   F   7. The easternmost provincial capital city is St. John's.

T   F   8. Cape Breton Island is part of Nova Scotia.

T   F   9. The city of Toronto is on Lake Erie.

T   F   10. Victoria Island lies directly north of Quebec.

T   F   11. The city of Ottawa is in the province of Ontario.

T   F   12. The city of Edmonton is northeast of the city of Winnipeg.

T   F   13. Baffin Island is the largest island in the Northwest Territories.

T   F   14. Prince Albert National Park is in the province of Saskatchewan.

T   F   15. Mount Logan, the highest mountain in Canada, is in British Columbia.

Name _____

O Canada

Look at a map of Canada to help you identify the **province** or **territory** that fits each description below. Use the names listed in the answer box at the bottom of the page to help you. You will need to use each province or territory only once.

1. westernmost province   _____

2. home of Lake Nipigon   _____

3. neighbor to Alaska but not Idaho   _____

4. province bordered on the east by the Labrador Sea   _____

5. province located east of the Bay of Fundy   _____

6. vast region that stretches north of the Arctic Circle   _____

7. province directly west of Manitoba   _____

8. home of the Birch Mountains and the Caribou Mountains   _____

9. neighbor to Maine but not New Hampshire   _____

10. province in which the largest lake and the capital city have the same name   _____

11. island province bordered on the south by the Northumberland Strait   _____

12. location of the Gaspé Peninsula   _____

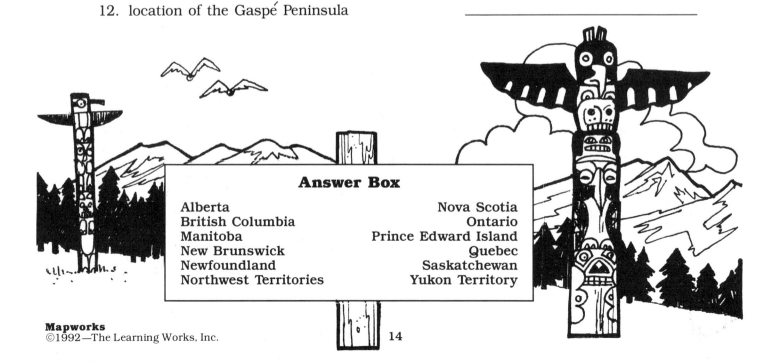

Answer Box

Alberta	Nova Scotia
British Columbia	Ontario
Manitoba	Prince Edward Island
New Brunswick	Quebec
Newfoundland	Saskatchewan
Northwest Territories	Yukon Territory

Continental Quest

Use a world map or a globe to identify the continents which fit the descriptions below. Use the letters in the box when you write your answers.

A	Africa	**D**	Australia
B	Antarctica	**E**	Europe
C	Asia	**F**	North America
	G South America		

In my quest I found the continent(s) which

1. border the Indian Ocean. _____

2. has the largest area. _____

3. touch no other continent. _____

4. contains the cities of Caracas and La Paz. _____

5. is home to the Altai Mountains and the Syrian Desert. _____

6. are crossed by the equator. _____

7. lie completely north of the equator. _____

8. lie completely south of the equator. _____

9. borders the Gulf of Honduras and the Hudson Bay. _____

10. contains the large cities of Brisbane and Perth. _____

11. is bordered by the Bay of Bengal and the Sea of Okhotsk. _____

12. lies directly south of the Weddell Sea and the Ross Sea. _____

13. contains the Balkan Peninsula and the Iberian Peninsula. _____

14. is home to Uruguay and French Guiana. _____

15. contains the countries of Ethiopia and Liberia. _____

Name _____

International Anagrams

> An **anagram** is a word or phrase that is created by rearranging all of the letters of another word or phrase. For example, the word *rain* is an anagram for *Iran.*

The words and phrases below are anagrams for the names of twelve countries. Unscramble each anagram. Write the name of the country in the first column and the name of the capital city in the second column.

Use the country names in the box at the bottom of the page to help you unscramble the anagrams, but be careful. You will not need *all* of the names in the box.

	Country	Capital City
1. plane	_____	_____
2. neat grain	_____	_____
3. own ray	_____	_____
4. sane leg	_____	_____
5. hand tail	_____	_____
6. age rail	_____	_____
7. dollar vase	_____	_____
8. oil a comb	_____	_____
9. bug mile	_____	_____
10. giant has fan	_____	_____
11. vine mat	_____	_____
12. agate alum	_____	_____

Country Names

Afghanistan	El Salvador	Norway
Algeria	Guatemala	Rwanda
Argentina	Italy	Senegal
Belgium	Nepal	Thailand
Colombia	Nicaragua	Vietnam

Name _____

Match-Mates

Each pair of cities listed below can be found in the same country. First, identify the country *outside of the United States* in which you would find both cities. Next, use the box at the bottom of the page to find the name of a third city located in that country. Finally, write the name of the third city and of the country in which all three cities can be found.

		Country	**City**
1. Cairo	Suez	_____	_____
2. Naples	Verona	_____	_____
3. Brisbane	Canberra	_____	_____
4. Osaka	Tokyo	_____	_____
5. Barcelona	Madrid	_____	_____
6. Salzburg	Vienna	_____	_____
7. Haifa	Tel Aviv	_____	_____
8. Paris	Rouen	_____	_____
9. Montreal	Ottawa	_____	_____
10. Mecca	Riyadh	_____	_____
11. Bombay	Calcutta	_____	_____
12. Acapulco	Guadalajara	_____	_____
13. Rio de Janeiro	São Paulo	_____	_____
14. Berlin	Munich	_____	_____
15. St. Petersburg (formerly Leningrad)	Novosibirsk	_____	_____

City Names

Aswan	Innsbruck	Mazatlán
Brasília	Jerusalem	Melbourne
Cartagena	Jiddah	Moscow
Frankfurt	Kyoto	New Delhi
Genoa	Marseille	Vancouver

Name _____

On the Border

Each pair of countries listed below shares a border with a third country.
Use a map or globe to help you identify the missing country.

1. Bangladesh _____ Thailand

2. Belgium _____ Italy

3. Kenya _____ Zambia

4. Bulgaria _____ Syria

5. Honduras _____ Mexico

6. Algeria _____ Guinea

7. France _____ Portugal

8. Hungary _____ Switzerland

9. Chad _____ Mali

10. Norway _____ Sweden

11. Nicaragua _____ Panama

12. Chile _____ Ecuador

13. Guyana _____ Venezuela

14. Jordan _____ Oman

15. Gabon _____ Zaire

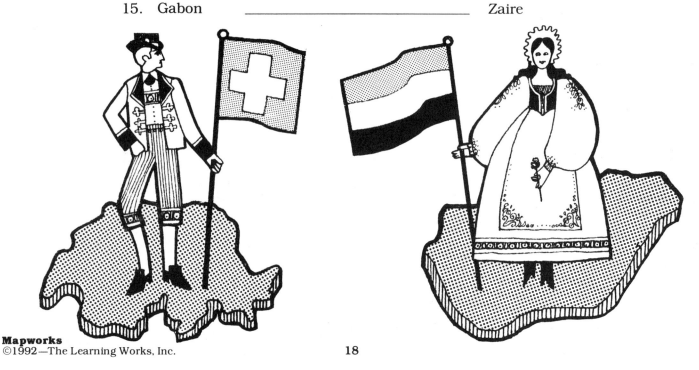

Name _____

All Wet!

Match each description in **Column A** with the correct body of water named in **Column B**.

Column A	**Column B**
_____ 1. between Tierra del Fuego and mainland South America	A. Gulf of Carpentaria
_____ 2. between Vietnam and the Philippines	B. Persian Gulf
_____ 3. between Yemen and Somalia	C. Gulf of Guinea
_____ 4. between Morocco and Spain	D. Strait of Gibraltar
_____ 5. between Singapore and Sumatra	E. Red Sea
_____ 6. southern part of Hudson Bay	F. South China Sea
_____ 7. between Saudi Arabia and Iran	G. James Bay
_____ 8. between Sweden and Finland	H. Bay of Biscay
_____ 9. between Egypt and Saudi Arabia	I. Gulf of Mexico
_____ 10. between Tasmania and mainland Australia	J. Gulf of Aden
_____ 11. north of Spain	K. Strait of Malacca
_____ 12. south of Nigeria	L. Bass Strait
_____ 13. between Iceland and Greenland	M. Denmark Strait
_____ 14. south of Louisiana and east of Mexico	N. Gulf of Bothnia
_____ 15. between Cape York Peninsula and the Northern Territory of Australia	O. Strait of Magellan

Oceans of Information

Use a globe or a map of the world to help you locate the countries and continents below. Write the correct letter or letters to show which of the oceans border the places listed.

A	Arctic Ocean	**C**	Indian Ocean
B	Atlantic Ocean	**D**	Pacific Ocean
	E	None of the above	

1. United States   _____

2. Chile   _____

3. Australia   _____

4. Antarctica   _____

5. Portugal   _____

6. Italy   _____

7. Japan   _____

8. Uruguay   _____

9. Nigeria   _____

10. Iraq   _____

11. Brazil   _____

12. Mexico   _____

13. Greenland   _____

14. India   _____

15. Switzerland   _____

Name _____

Island Groups

Use a world map to find each of the island groups listed below. Match each island group to the body of water in which it is located by writing the correct letter on each line.

A	Arctic Ocean	**D**	Indian Ocean
B	Atlantic Ocean	**E**	Mediterranean Sea
C	Caribbean Sea	**F**	Pacific Ocean

1. the Azores _____

2. Society Islands _____

3. Galapagos Islands _____

4. Falkland Islands _____

5. the Grenadines _____

6. Seychelles _____

7. Canary Islands _____

8. Balearic Islands _____

9. Mariana Islands _____

10. Madeira Islands _____

11. Queen Elizabeth Islands _____

12. the Maldives _____

13. Line Islands _____

14. Midway Islands _____

15. Cayman Islands _____

Name _____

Island Paradise

Use a map of the world to identify each island listed below. Write the name of the island on the line beside each description.

This island is

1. the largest in Hawaii. _____

2. directly south of Australia. _____

3. closest to the "toe" of Italy. _____

4. south of Turkey and directly west of Syria. _____

5. directly east of the Formosa Strait. _____

6. separated from the east coast of Africa by the Mozambique Channel. _____

7. separated from Greenland by the Denmark Strait. _____

8. the largest in the Philippines. _____

9. the home of the capital of British Columbia. _____

10. directly southeast of India. _____

11. southeast of Australia. _____

12. shared by Haiti and the Dominican Republic. _____

13. the largest island in the Gulf of Alaska. _____

14. in the Mediterranean Sea north of Sardinia. _____

15. directly south of the Strait of Magellan. _____

Name _____

From Sea to Shining Sea

Each pair of countries below is linked by a sea. Use a map or a globe to identify the two countries and the sea that lies between them. Write the name of the sea on the line between the countries.

1. Jordan _____ Israel

2. India _____ Oman

3. Japan _____ North Korea

4. Cuba _____ Colombia

5. Italy _____ Libya

6. Norway _____ Iceland

7. Greece _____ Turkey

8. Denmark _____ Great Britain

9. Sudan _____ Saudi Arabia

10. China _____ South Korea

11. Turkey _____ Ukraine

12. Sweden _____ Latvia

13. Russia _____ USA (Southern Alaska)

14. Canada _____ Greenland

15. Australia _____ New Zealand

Name _____

World Rivers

Use an almanac, an atlas, or an encyclopedia to find the length and continental home of each of the twelve rivers listed in the box below. Complete the chart by listing the rivers in order **from longest to shortest**.

	River	Continent	Length
1.			
2.			
3.			
4.			
5.			
6.			
7.			
8.			
9.			
10.			
11.			
12.			

River Names

Amazon	Ganges	Niger
Columbia	Huang	Nile
Danube	Mackenzie	Volga
Euphrates	Mississippi	Yukon

Name _____

Higher Than the Highest Mountain

Use an almanac, an atlas, or an encyclopedia to find the height and continental home of each of the twelve mountains listed in the box below. Complete the chart by listing the mountains in order **from highest to lowest**.

	Mountain	Continent	Height
1.			
2.			
3.			
4.			
5.			
6.			
7.			
8.			
9.			
10.			
11.			
12.			

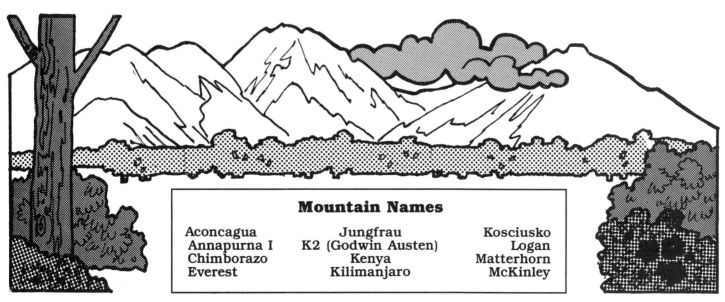

Mountain Names

Aconcagua	Jungfrau	Kosciusko
Annapurna I	K2 (Godwin Austen)	Logan
Chimborazo	Kenya	Matterhorn
Everest	Kilimanjaro	McKinley

Name _____

High & Dry

Match the mountain ranges and deserts in the first column with the locations listed in the second column. Use a world map or an encyclopedia to help you.

_____ 1. Apennines

_____ 2. Atacama Desert

_____ 3. Atlas Mountains

_____ 4. Caucasus Mountains

_____ 5. Pyrenees Mountains

_____ 6. Cascade Mountains

_____ 7. Brooks Range

_____ 8. Gobi Desert

_____ 9. Queen Maud Mountains

_____ 10. Great Sandy Desert

_____ 11. the Himalayas

_____ 12. Kalahari Desert

_____ 13. Appalachian Mountains

_____ 14. Great Dividing Range

_____ 15. Sahara Desert

A. Algeria and Morocco

B. eastern United States

C. Italy

D. between the Black Sea and the Caspian Sea

E. northern Chile

F. southern Africa

G. China and Mongolia

H. northern Africa, from the Atlantic Ocean to the Red Sea

I. eastern Australia

J. Alaska

K. on the border between France and Spain

L. western Australia

M. China, India, and Nepal

N. California, Oregon, and Washington

O. Antarctica

Name _____

Physically Fit

Physical features such as capes, islands, lakes, mountains, peninsulas, and rivers give the land its characteristic form and shape. Using the list of physical features below, match each feature to the continent on which it is located.

Africa

_____
_____
_____

Antarctica

_____
_____
_____

Asia

_____
_____
_____

Australia

Europe

_____
_____
_____

North America

_____
_____
_____

South America

_____
_____
_____

Physical Features

Alps	Ionian Islands	Parry Islands
Cape of Good Hope	Lake Eyre	Queen Maud Land
Cape Horn	Lake Superior	Rockefeller Plateau
Cape York Peninsula	Malay Peninsula	Rocky Mountains
Congo River	Mekong River Delta	Ross Ice Shelf
Darling River	Mount Ararat	Tiber River
Guiana Highlands	Orinoco River	Zambezi River

Name _____

Line Up

> To help us find where places are on the earth, mapmakers have created a system of lines. Map lines that run east and west are called **lines of latitude**. Lines of latitude measure the distance north or south of the **equator**, which is 0° latitude. Map lines that run north and south are called **lines of longitude**. Lines of longitude measure the distance east or west of the **prime meridian**, which is 0° longitude.

Find each line of latitude or longitude on a world map or a globe. Circle the name of the place in each pair through which the line of latitude or longitude crosses.

Latitude			**Longitude**		
1. 20° N	India	Iran	8. 100° E	Thailand	Vietnam
2. 40° S	Brazil	Argentina	9. 60° W	Paraguay	Uruguay
3. 60° N	Sweden	Poland	10. 20° W	Atlantic Ocean	Pacific Ocean
4. 20° S	Australia	New Zealand	11. 0°	France	Portugal
5. 80° N	Iceland	Greenland	12. 140° W	Bering Sea	Beaufort Sea
6. 30° S	Bolivia	Chile	13. 100° W	Nebraska	Iowa
7. 0°	Nigeria	Kenya	14. 140° E	Korea	Japan

Name _____

As the Crow Flies

> Using a **map scale** is a way of estimating distances between points on a map. Most maps are small in comparison to the area they represent. Maps are drawn "to scale," so that the distance on the map corresponds to a specific distance on the earth. For example, one inch on a map might represent one hundred miles on the earth.

Use the map scale on a world map to find the **country** or **body of water** which is 500 miles in the direction indicated from each place below. Remember that map scales vary, so be careful to check each scale if you use more than one map.

What country or body of water is 500 miles

1. east of Rio de Janeiro, Brazil?   _____

2. southeast of Canberra, Australia?   _____

3. south of Dallas, Texas?   _____

4. south of Santa Fe, New Mexico?   _____

5. west of Bombay, India?   _____

6. east of Helsinki, Finland?   _____

7. northwest of Oslo, Norway?   _____

8. east of Port Elizabeth, South Africa?   _____

9. south of Nairobi, Kenya?   _____

10. northeast of Asunción, Paraguay?   _____

11. north of Panama City, Panama?   _____

12. east of Jerusalem, Israel?   _____

13. west of Dublin, Ireland?   _____

14. west of Lima, Peru?   _____

15. east of Fairbanks, Alaska?   _____

Name _____

A Closer Look: Africa

Take "a closer look" at a detailed map of Africa to help you decide if each of the statements below is correct. Circle **T** if the statement is **true** and **F** if the statement is **false**.

T   F   1. The tiny nation of Lesotho lies within the borders of South Africa.

T   F   2. The island of Madagascar lies off the coast of Angola.

T   F   3. Tanzania and Uganda border Lake Victoria.

T   F   4. Kilimanjaro is in Mozambique.

T   F   5. The equator crosses Kenya.

T   F   6. The Suez Canal is located in Sudan.

T   F   7. The Limpopo River separates South Africa from Zimbabwe.

T   F   8. The country of Niger borders the Gulf of Guinea.

T   F   9. Tunisia is bordered by the Mediterranean Sea.

T   F   10. The Kalahari Desert is in Botswana.

T   F   11. Lake Tanganyika lies on the eastern border of Tanzania.

T   F   12. The Canary Islands lie off the western coast of Mauritania.

T   F   13. Both the Tropic of Cancer and the Tropic of Capricorn cross Africa.

T   F   14. Lake Volta can be found in Ghana.

T   F   15. Uganda is south of Sudan.

Name _____

A Closer Look: Asia

Take "a closer look" at a detailed map of Asia to help you identify the country which either contains or borders *both* of the geographical locations listed below. Write the name of the country in the first column and the name of its capital in the second column.

	Country	Capital City
1. Yangtze River, Yellow Sea		
2. Indus River, Khyber Pass		
3. Da Nang, Gulf of Tonkin		
4. Persian Gulf, Rub al Khali		
5. Dead Sea, Negev Desert		
6. Lake Baykal, Laptev Sea		
7. Kyushu, Mount Fuji		
8. Arabian Sea, Ganges River		
9. Luzon, South China Sea		
10. Caspian Sea, Zagros Mountains		
11. Pusan, Yellow Sea		
12. Kuwait, Tigris River		
13. Java, Kapuas River		
14. Dead Sea, Iraq		
15. Gobi Desert, Selenge River		

Name _____

A Closer Look: Australia

Take "a closer look" at a detailed map of Australia to help you match the descriptions in the first column to the place names in the second column. Be careful! You should use each place name only once, and you will not need all of them.

_____ 1. body of water which lies off the western coast of Australia

_____ 2. the largest state

_____ 3. the national capital

_____ 4. state containing Cape York Peninsula

_____ 5. line of latitude which crosses Australia

_____ 6. largest coral formation in the world, located off the coast of Queensland

_____ 7. state in which Melbourne is located

_____ 8. large arid region in Western Australia

_____ 9. body of water between Australia and New Zealand

_____ 10. island state

_____ 11. the highest point in Australia

_____ 12. state in which Sydney is located

A. Mount Kosciusko

B. Pacific Ocean

C. Great Barrier Reef

D. Western Australia

E. Great Sandy Desert

F. Tropic of Cancer

G. Indian Ocean

H. Tasmania

I. New South Wales

J. Ayers Rock

K. Victoria

L. Tropic of Capricorn

M. Queensland

N. Tasman Sea

O. Canberra

Name _____

A Closer Look: Europe

Take "a closer look" at a detailed map of Europe to help you identify each of the places described below. Write the correct place name on the line next to its description.

1. These mountains separate France and Spain. _____

2. England, Scotland, and Wales are located on this island. _____

3. The Rhône River flows through this country to the Mediterranean Sea. _____

4. This country's capital city is Sofia. _____

5. Denmark is separated from Great Britain by this sea. _____

6. This river runs through the capital of France. _____

7. The westernmost and northernmost European capital city is in this country. _____

8. This mountain range runs from the Gulf of Genoa to the "toe" of Italy. _____

9. Nine countries touch this European nation's borders. _____

10. This sea separates Greece and Turkey. _____

11. The Strait of Gibraltar separates this country from Africa. _____

12. This country on the Baltic Sea is bordered by Germany, Lithuania, and Ukraine. _____

13. Belgium, France, and Germany surround this tiny country. _____

14. This body of water lies between Finland and Sweden. _____

15. This river passes through three European capitals. _____

Name _____

A Closer Look: North America

Take "a closer look" at a detailed map of North America to help you identify each of the places described below. Write the correct place name on
the line next to its description.

1. strait between Florida and Cuba _____

2. bay between Greenland and Baffin Island _____

3. sea between Alaska and the North Pole _____

4. country bordered by Coronado Bay _____

5. capital of Jamaica _____

6. country whose capital is Tegucigalpa _____

7. gulf north of Prince Edward Island _____

8. sea between southern Alaska and Russia _____

9. largest lake in Central America _____

10. country bordered by Mexico and Guatemala _____

11. country in which the Catskill Mountains are
located _____

12. sea between northern Alaska and Russia _____

13. highest point in Mexico _____

14. largest North American country crossed by
the Tropic of Cancer _____

15. place in the United States with the lowest
elevation _____

A Closer Look: South America

Take "a closer look" at a detailed map of South America to help you identify each of the places described below. Write the correct place name on
the line next to its description.

1. capital of Chile _____

2. country directly west of the Falkland Islands _____

3. the longest mountain range in the world,
   stretching from Colombia to Cape Horn _____

4. the only South American country to border
   Central America _____

5. the two landlocked countries in South America _____

   _____

6. lake on the border between Peru and Bolivia _____

7. longest river in South America, carrying more
   water than any other river in the world _____

8. sea which lies north of South America _____

9. country containing Aconcagua, the highest
   peak on the continent _____

10. country in which Angel Falls is located _____

11. continent separated from South America by
    Drake Passage _____

12. the largest lake in South America, located in
    Venezuela _____

Name _____

Order, Please!

Rank each of the three locations in the series below. Write the number **1** on the line next to the largest, highest, longest, or deepest place in the group. Write the number **2** by the mid-sized location and the number **3** next to the smallest, lowest, shortest, or shallowest of the three.

1. **area** ____ Idaho ____ Indiana ____ Iowa

2. **area** ____ Arctic Ocean ____ Atlantic Ocean ____ Indian Ocean

3. **height** ____ Angel Falls ____ Ribbon Falls ____ Victoria Falls

4. **area** ____ Africa ____ North America ____ South America

5. **area** ____ Bahrain ____ Jamaica ____ New Guinea

6. **height** ____ Mauna Loa ____ Mount St. Helens ____ Mount Vesuvius

7. **area** ____ Kara Kum ____ Mojave Desert ____ Sahara Desert

8. **area** ____ Lake Huron ____ Lake Michigan ____ Lake Ontario

9. **height** ____ Mount Rainier ____ Mount Shasta ____ Pikes Peak

10. **population** ____ Chicago ____ Hong Kong ____ Mexico City

11. **area** ____ Georgia ____ New York ____ Pennsylvania

12. **population** ____ Japan ____ United Kingdom ____ United States

13. **area** ____ Antarctica ____ Australia ____ Europe

14. **length** ____ Loire River ____ Rio de la Plata ____ Rio Grande

15. **average depth** ____ Atlantic Ocean ____ Indian Ocean ____ Pacific Ocean

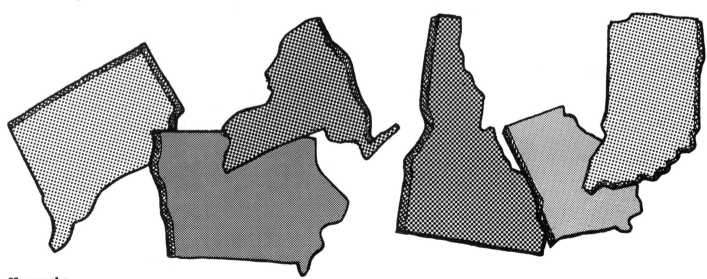

Big Deal!

Use an almanac, atlas, encyclopedia or world record book to identify these largest and highest places.

1. largest island _____

2. largest desert _____

3. highest waterfall _____

4. largest lake _____

5. largest ocean _____

6. largest continent _____

7. largest Great Lake _____

8. highest point in North America _____

9. largest state east of the Mississipi _____

10. largest city in the United States (population) _____

11. largest country (area) _____

12. largest country (population) _____

13. largest country in Africa (area) _____

14. highest mountain in Europe _____

15. largest island in the Philippines _____

Four-Letter Geography

Each description below fits a place with four letters in its name. Use the clues to help you identify each place.

1. state north of Missouri   — — — —

2. country east of Niger   — — — —

3. largest continent   — — — —

4. island nation directly south of Florida   — — — —

5. capital of Italy   — — — —

6. island home of Hawaii's capital city   — — — —

7. state separating Indiana and Pennsylvania   — — — —

8. canal in Egypt   — — — —

9. capital of Ukraine   — — — —

10. African nation between Mauritania and Niger   — — — —

11. country whose capital is Lima   — — — —

12. small country between Ghana and Benin   — — — —

13. capital of Switzerland   — — — —

14. country which borders Cambodia and
    Vietnam   — — — —

15. country between the Caspian Sea and the
    Persian Gulf   — — — —

Name _____

Misfits

Three of the four places in each numbered row have something in common and belong together. Find the place that does *not* belong and underline it. Use the answer box at the bottom of the page to find the name of a place that *does* belong to the group of three places. Write the name of the fourth place on the line beside each list.

1. Bolivia /Mexico /Paraguay /Peru   _____

2. Lisbon /Madrid /Prague /Tokyo   _____

3. Italy /Pakistan /Thailand /Vietnam   _____

4. Boston /Chicago /Helena /Sacramento   _____

5. Estonia /Kazakhstan /Myanmar /Ukraine   _____

6. Cuba /Grenada /Jamaica /Taiwan   _____

7. Greece /Netherlands /Qatar /Romania   _____

8. Adirondacks /Carpathians /Sierra Leone /Urals   _____

9. Crete /Cyprus /Ireland /Sicily   _____

10. Bali /Chad /Rwanda /Somalia   _____

11. Berlin / Liechtenstein /Monaco /San Marino   _____

12. Alberta /Montreal /Nova Scotia /Saskatchewan   _____

Answer Box

Andorra	Ecuador	Ottawa
Austin	Ghana	Quebec
Biloxi	India	Sierra Nevada
Barbados	Latvia	Stromboli
Caspian Sea	New Delhi	Tasman Sea
Corsica	Norway	Vienna

Geography ABCs

Each of the descriptions below fits a geographical location with five letters. Complete the geographical alphabet by filling in the remaining letters of each description.

1. mountain range in western South America   A _ _ _ _

2. African nation directly east of Togo   B _ _ _ _

3. country west of Argentina   C _ _ _ _

4. capital of Delaware   D _ _ _ _

5. country in which the Nile Delta is located   E _ _ _ _

6. Michigan city between Pontiac and Saginaw   F _ _ _ _

7. country east of Ivory Coast   G _ _ _ _

8. neighbor to the Dominican Republic on the island of
   Hispaniola   H _ _ _ _

9. country between the Bay of Bengal and the Arabian Sea   I _ _ _ _

10. island nation east of North Korea and South Korea   J _ _ _ _

11. country on the eastern coast of Africa   K _ _ _ _

12. African nation bordering the Mediterranean Sea   L _ _ _ _

Geography ABCs
(continued)

13. New England state bordering only one other state   M _ _ _ _

14. country directly north of India   N _ _ _ _

15. plateau in southern Missouri and northern Arkansas   O _ _ _ _

16. capital of France   P _ _ _ _

17. capital of Ecuador   Q _ _ _ _

18. river on the border between France and Germany   R _ _ _ _

19. country north of Jordan   S _ _ _ _

20. capital of Japan   T _ _ _ _

21. New York city east of Syracuse   U _ _ _ _

22. river flowing into the Caspian Sea   V _ _ _ _

23. country on the west coast of Great Britain   W _ _ _ _

24. Ohio town southeast of Dayton   X _ _ _ _

25. country north of the Gulf of Aden   Y _ _ _ _

26. country east of Congo   Z _ _ _ _

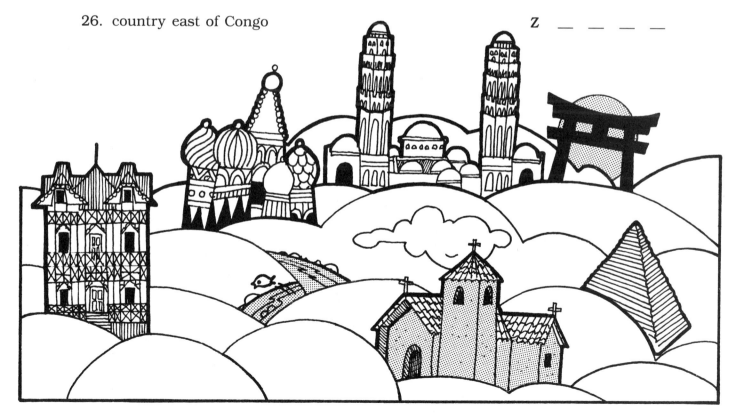

Name _____

Cross-Country

What country would you cross if you flew in a straight line from

1. Belgrade, Yugoslavia, to Vienna, Austria? _____

2. Brasilia, Brazil, to Lima, Peru? _____

3. Baghdad, Iraq, to Kabul, Afghanistan? _____

4. Belmopan, Belize, to Mexico City, Mexico? _____

5. London, England, to Stockholm, Sweden? _____

6. Kathmandu, Nepal, to Ulan Bator, Mongolia? _____

7. Algiers, Algeria, to Tripoli, Libya? _____

8. Athens, Greece, to Bucharest, Romania? _____

9. Caracas, Venezuela, to Quito, Ecuador? _____

10. Bern, Switzerland, to Madrid, Spain? _____

11. Bangkok, Thailand, to Hanoi, Vietnam? _____

12. Havana, Cuba, to San Salvador, El Salvador? _____

13. Brazzaville, Congo, to Yaoundé, Cameroon? _____

14. Jakarta, Indonesia, to Wellington, New Zealand? _____

15. Helsinki, Finland, to Riga, Latvia? _____

From Start to Finish

Each geographic feature described below begins and ends with the letter **A**. Use the clues to help you identify the features, and write the missing letters on the lines.

1. Canadian province west of Saskatchewan   A __ __ __ __ __ A

2. African nation east of Morocco   A __ __ __ __ __ A

3. country west of Hungary   A __ __ __ __ __ A

4. capital of Ghana   A __ __ __ A

5. former Soviet republic whose capital is Yerevan   A __ __ __ __ __ A

6. state whose capital is Montgomery   A __ __ __ __ __ A

7. small country between France and Spain   A __ __ __ __ __ A

8. capital of Turkey   A __ __ __ __ A

9. nation west of Uruguay   A __ __ __ __ __ __ __ A

10. mountain in Nepal   A __ __ __ __ __ __ A

11. country directly north of Greece   A __ __ __ __ __ A

12. nation west of Zambia   A __ __ __ __ A

13. sea between New Guinea and Australia   A __ __ __ __ __ A

14. capital city of Guam   A __ __ __ A

15. capital of the state which is north of Florida   A __ __ __ __ __ A

Mapworks
Completion Chart

1																			
2																			
3																			
4																			
5																			
6																			
7																			
8																			
9																			
10																			
11																			
12																			
13																			
14																			
15																			
16																			
17																			
18																			
19																			
20																			
21																			
22																			
23																			
24																			
25																			
26																			
27																			
28																			
29																			
30																			

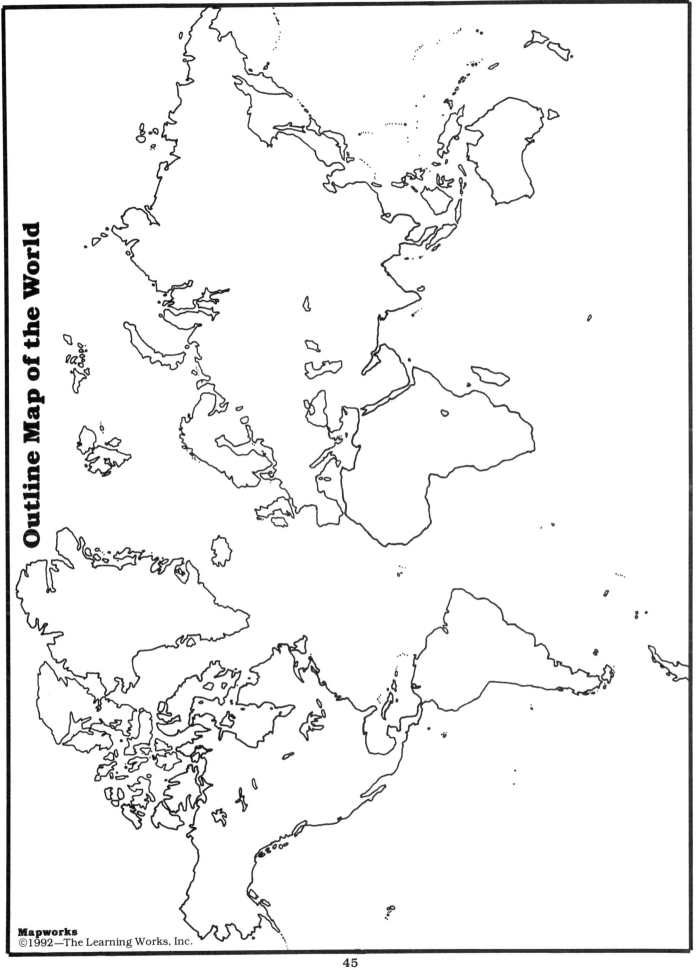

Answer Key

Page 5, Which State Am I?
1. South Dakota
2. Washington
3. Wyoming
4. Delaware
5. Florida
6. Wisconsin
7. Maine
8. Alaska
9. New York
10. Massachusetts
11. California
12. Montana
13. Tennessee or Missouri
14. Arizona
15. Mississippi

Page 6, Neighborly Trios
1. Oregon
2. Kentucky
3. Colorado
4. Utah
5. Nebraska
6. Minnesota
7. West Virginia
8. Arkansas
9. South Dakota
10. New Hampshire
11. Illinois
12. Idaho
13. Georgia
14. Ohio
15. Alabama

Page 7, On Opposite Sides
1. Mississippi
2. Colorado
3. Mississippi
4. Sabine
5. Ohio
6. Red River of the North, or Red River
7. Potomac
8. Delaware
9. Connecticut
10. Savannah
11. Columbia
12. Wabash
13. Snake
14. Red
15. Missouri

Page 8, Count Me Out
Cross out the following locations:
1. Devils Tower (WY)
2. Chesapeake Bay (MD / VA)
3. Mobile Bay (AL)
4. Lake Winnebago (WI)
5. White Sands National Monument (NM)
6. Cape Cod (MA)
7. Mesabi Range (MN)
8. Green Mountains (VT)
9. Zion National Park (UT)
10. Acadia National Park (ME)
11. Badlands (SD)
12. Grand Coulee Dam (WA)
13. Ouachita Mountains (AR-OK)
14. Pamlico Sound (NC)
15. Flathead Lake (MT)

Page 9, Capital Anagrams
1. Bismarck, ND
2. Harrisburg, PA
3. Nashville, TN
4. Little Rock, AR
5. Baton Rouge, LA
6. Providence, RI
7. Annapolis, MD
8. Tallahassee, FL
9. Sacramento, CA
10. Indianapolis, IN
11. Montpelier, VT
12. Oklahoma City, OK

Page 10, Which Way?
1. NW
2. NE
3. NW
4. N
5. SE
6. SW
7. SW
8. E
9. NE
10. W
11. SE
12. NE
13. NW
14. SE
15. SW

Page 11, Where Am I?
1. Florida
2. South Dakota
3. Alaska
4. Oklahoma
5. Oregon
6. New Mexico
7. Missouri
8. Nevada
9. North Carolina
10. Minnesota
11. Maine
12. Pennsylvania
13. Idaho
14. Indiana
15. Wisconsin

Page 12, Miles to Go
1. 500
2. 400
3. 1,000
4. 800
5. 750
6. 800
7. 600
8. 500
9. 700
10. 1,250
11. 600
12. 800

Page 13, Ten are True
1. T
2. T
3. F
4. T
5. T
6. T
7. T
8. T
9. F
10. F
11. T
12. F
13. T
14. T
15. F

Page 14, O Canada
1. British Columbia
2. Ontario
3. Yukon Territory
4. Newfoundland
5. Nova Scotia
6. Northwest Territories
7. Saskatchewan
8. Alberta
9. New Brunswick
10. Manitoba
11. Prince Edward Island
12. Quebec

Page 15, Continental Quest
1. A, B, C, D
2. C
3. B, D
4. G
5. C
6. A, C, G
7. E, F
8. B, D
9. F
10. D
11. C
12. B
13. E
14. G
15. A

Page 16, International Anagrams
1. Nepal, Kathmandu
2. Argentina, Buenos Aires
3. Norway, Oslo
4. Senegal, Dakar
5. Thailand, Bangkok
6. Algeria, Algiers
7. El Salvador, San Salvador
8. Colombia, Bogotá
9. Belgium, Brussels
10. Afghanistan, Kabul
11. Vietnam, Hanoi
12. Guatemala, Guatemala (City)

Page 17, Match-Mates
1. Egypt, Aswân
2. Italy, Genoa
3. Australia, Melbourne
4. Japan, Kyoto
5. Spain, Cartagena
6. Austria, Innsbruck
7. Israel, Jerusalem
8. France, Marseille
9. Canada, Vancouver
10. Saudi Arabia, Jiddah
11. India, New Delhi
12. Mexico, Mazatlán
13. Brazil, Brasília
14. Germany, Frankfurt
15. Russia, Moscow

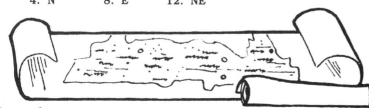

Answer Key
(Continued)

Page 18, On the Border
1. Myanmar (Burma)
2. France
3. Tanzania
4. Turkey
5. Guatemala
6. Mali
7. Spain
8. Austria
9. Niger
10. Finland
11. Costa Rica
12. Peru
13. Brazil
14. Saudi Arabia
15. Congo

Page 19, All Wet!
1. O
2. F
3. J
4. D
5. K
6. G
7. B
8. N
9. E
10. L
11. H
12. C
13. M
14. I
15. A

Page 20, Oceans of Information
1. A, B, D
2. D
3. C, D
4. B, C, D
5. B
6. E
7. D
8. B
9. B
10. E
11. B
12. D
13. A, B
14. C
15. E

Page 21, Island Groups
1. B
2. F
3. F
4. B
5. C
6. D
7. B
8. E
9. F
10. B
11. A
12. D
13. F
14. F
15. C

Page 22, Island Paradise
1. Hawaii
2. Tasmania
3. Sicily
4. Cyprus
5. Taiwan
6. Madagascar
7. Iceland
8. Luzon
9. Vancouver Island
10. Sri Lanka
11. New Zealand
12. Hispaniola
13. Kodiak Island
14. Corsica
15. Tierra del Fuego

Page 23, From Sea to Shining Sea
1. Dead Sea
2. Arabian Sea
3. Sea of Japan
4. Caribbean Sea
5. Mediterranean Sea
6. Norwegian Sea
7. Aegean Sea
8. North Sea
9. Red Sea
10. Yellow Sea
11. Black Sea
12. Baltic Sea
13. Bering Sea
14. Labrador Sea
15. Tasman Sea

Page 24, World Rivers
River lengths may vary depending on the resource used. Some sources consider the Amazon to be the longest river in the world (4,195 mi.).

1.	Nile	Africa	4,160 mi.
2.	Amazon	South America	4,000 mi.
3.	Huang	Asia	2,903 mi.
4.	Mackenzie	North America	2,635 mi.
5.	Niger	Africa	2,590 mi.
6.	Mississippi	North America	2,340 mi.
7.	Volga	Europe	2,194 mi.
8.	Yukon	North America	1,979 mi.
9.	Danube	Europe	1,776 mi.
10.	Euphrates	Asia	1,700 mi.
11.	Ganges	Asia	1,560 mi.
12.	Columbia	North America	1,243 mi.

Page 25, Higher Than the Highest Mountain
Mountain heights may vary depending on the resource used.

1.	Everest	Asia	29,028 ft.
2.	K2	Asia	28,250 ft.
3.	Annapurna I	Asia	26,504 ft.
4.	Aconcagua	South America	22,834 ft.
5.	Chimborazo	South America	20,561 ft.
6.	McKinley	North America	20,320 ft.
7.	Logan	North America	19,850 ft.
8.	Kilimanjaro	Africa	19,340 ft.
9.	Kenya	Africa	17,058 ft.
10.	Matterhorn	Europe	14,690 ft.
11.	Jungfrau	Europe	13,642 ft.
12.	Kosciusko	Australia	7,310 ft.

Page 26, High & Dry
1. C
2. E
3. A
4. D
5. K
6. N
7. J
8. G
9. O
10. L
11. M
12. F
13. B
14. I
15. H

Page 27, Physically Fit
Africa: Cape of Good Hope, Congo River, Zambezi River
Antarctica: Queen Maud Land, Rockefeller Plateau, Ross Ice Shelf
Asia: Malay Peninsula, Mekong River Delta, Mount Ararat
Australia: Cape York Peninsula, Darling River, Lake Eyre
Europe: Alps, Ionian Islands, Tiber River
North America: Lake Superior, Parry Islands, Rocky Mountains
South America: Cape Horn, Guiana Highlands, Orinoco River

Page 28, Line Up
1. India
2. Argentina
3. Sweden
4. Australia
5. Greenland
6. Chile
7. Kenya
8. Thailand
9. Paraguay
10. Atlantic Ocean
11. France
12. Beaufort Sea
13. Nebraska
14. Japan

Page 29, As the Crow Flies
1. Atlantic Ocean
2. Tasman Sea
3. Gulf of Mexico
4. Mexico
5. Arabian Sea
6. Russia
7. Norwegian Sea
8. Indian Ocean
9. Tanzania
10. Brazil
11. Caribbean Sea
12. Iraq
13. Atlantic Ocean
14. Pacific Ocean
15. Canada

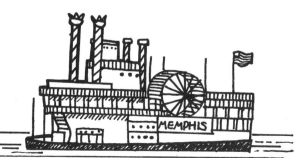

MEMPHIS

Answer Key
(Continued)

Page 30, A Closer Look: Africa
1. T	5. T	9. T	13. T
2. F	6. F	10. T	14. T
3. T	7. T	11. F	15. T
4. F	8. F	12. F	

Page 31, A Closer Look: Asia
1. China, Beijing
2. Pakistan, Islamabad
3. Vietnam, Hanoi
4. Saudi Arabia, Riyadh
5. Israel, Jerusalem
6. Russia, Moscow
7. Japan, Tokyo
8. India, New Delhi
9. Philippines, Manila
10. Iran, Tehran
11. South Korea, Seoul
12. Iraq, Baghdad
13. Indonesia, Jakarta
14. Jordan, Amman
15. Mongolia, Ulan Bator

Page 32, A Closer Look: Australia
1. G	4. M	7. K	10. H
2. D	5. L	8. E	11. A
3. O	6. C	9. N	12. I

Page 33, A Closer Look: Europe
1. Pyrenees
2. Great Britain
3. France
4. Bulgaria
5. North Sea
6. Seine
7. Iceland
8. Apennines
9. Germany
10. Aegean Sea
11. Spain
12. Poland
13. Luxembourg
14. Gulf of Bothnia
15. Danube

Page 34, A Closer Look: North America
1. Straits of Florida
2. Baffin Bay
3. Beaufort Sea
4. Costa Rica
5. Kingston
6. Honduras
7. Gulf of St. Lawrence
8. Bering Sea
9. Lake Nicaragua
10. Belize
11. United States
12. Chukchi Sea
13. Mount Orizaba
14. Mexico
15. Death Valley

Page 35, A Closer Look: South America
1. Santiago
2. Argentina
3. Andes
4. Colombia
5. Paraguay and Bolivia
6. Titicaca
7. Amazon
8. Caribbean
9. Argentina
10. Venezuela
11. Antarctica
12. Maracaibo

Page 36, Order, Please!
1. 1, 3, 2	6. 1, 2, 3	11. 1, 2, 3
2. 3, 1, 2	7. 2, 3, 1	12. 2, 3, 1
3. 1, 2, 3	8. 1, 2, 3	13. 1, 3, 2
4. 1, 2, 3	9. 1, 2, 3	14. 2, 3, 1
5. 3, 2, 1	10. 3, 2, 1	15. 3, 2, 1

Page 37, Big Deal!
1. Greenland
2. Sahara Desert
3. Angel Falls
4. Caspian Sea
5. Pacific Ocean
6. Asia
7. Lake Superior
8. Mt. McKinley
9. Georgia
10. New York City
11. Russia
12. China
13. Sudan
14. Mount Elbrus
15. Luzon

Page 38, Four-Letter Geography
1. Iowa	6. Oahu	11. Peru
2. Chad	7. Ohio	12. Togo
3. Asia	8. Suez	13. Bern
4. Cuba	9. Kiev	14. Laos
5. Rome	10. Mali	15. Iran

Page 39, Misfits
1. cross out Mexico; Ecuador
2. cross out Tokyo; Vienna
3. cross out Italy; India
4. cross out Chicago; Austin
5. cross out Myanmar; Latvia
6. cross out Taiwan; Barbados
7. cross out Qatar; Norway
8. cross out Sierra Leone; Sierra Nevada
9. cross out Ireland; Corsica
10. cross out Bali; Ghana
11. cross out Berlin; Andorra
12. cross out Montreal; Quebec

Pages 40-41, Geography ABCs
1. Andes	10. Japan	19. Syria
2. Benin	11. Kenya	20. Tokyo
3. Chile	12. Libya	21. Utica
4. Dover	13. Maine	22. Volga
5. Egypt	14. Nepal	23. Wales
6. Flint	15. Ozark	24. Xenia
7. Ghana	16. Paris	25. Yemen
8. Haiti	17. Quito	26. Zaire
9. India	18. Rhine	

Page 42, Cross-Country
1. Hungary	6. China	11. Laos
2. Bolivia	7. Tunisia	12. Honduras
3. Iran	8. Bulgaria	13. Gabon
4. Guatemala	9. Colombia	14. Australia
5. Denmark	10. France	15. Estonia

Page 43, From Start to Finish
1. Alberta	6. Alabama	11. Albania
2. Algeria	7. Andorra	12. Angola
3. Austria	8. Ankara	13. Arafura
4. Accra	9. Argentina	14. Agana
5. Armenia	10. Annapurna	15. Atlanta